for James, Rebecca and Sally Maidment

First published in the U.S.A. 1986 by E. P. Dutton,
a division of NAL Penguin Inc.
2 Park Avenue, New York, N.Y. 10016

Originally published in England 1986 by Andersen Press Limited,
62–65 Chandos Place, London WC2N 4NW

Copyright © 1986 by Ruth Brown

ISBN: 0-525-44256-1

Printed in Verona, Italy, by Grafiche AZ
10 9 8 7 6 5 4 3 2    OBE    First Edition

# Our Cat Flossie

## RUTH BROWN

E. P. DUTTON   NEW YORK

This is our cat Flossie.

She lives with us in the city.

She likes the house and the garden, but does not
get on very well with the neighbors.

Her hobbies include bird watching

and fishing.

Flossie is a skillful climber

and an enthusiastic gardener.

She always insists on helping with knitting

and making the beds.

She is very good at polishing shoes

but not quite so useful at Christmastime.

There are two things which she hates—
the sound of fireworks

and visits to the vet.

Flossie loves collecting butterflies

and she is rather fond of snails,

even though she finds them puzzling.

She is unable to resist a box

no matter what the size.

But like all cats, mostly she loves to sleep...

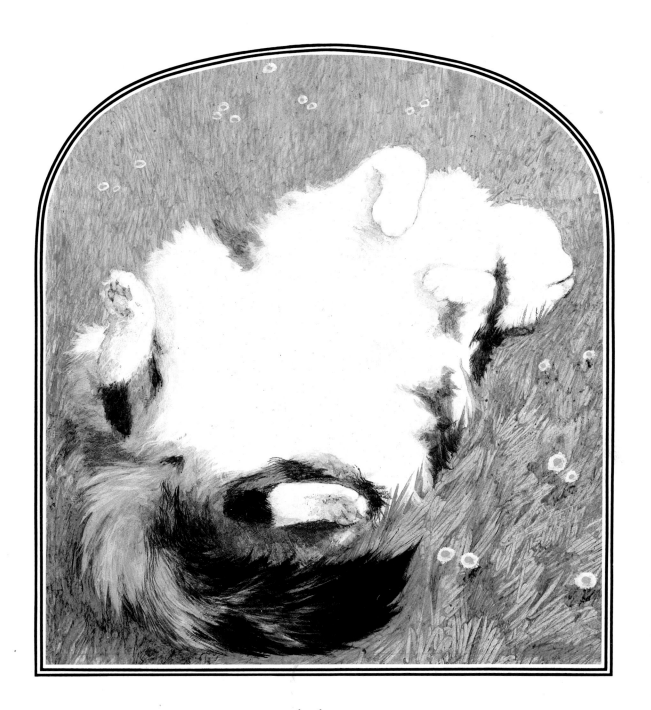

and sleep...

and sleep.